Then Bonzo jumped out of bed.

He stretched and yawned.

He said good morning to his family.

Big

Not-So-Big

Small

Tiny

Not-So-Big let him out into the garden, where he sniffed around.

Then he went in and had his usual breakfast.

After breakfast, Small took Bonzo
for a walk. It was always the same.

They would go along three streets
and up Lizard Lane.

Three cats lived along the route.
There were three reasons why
Bonzo didn't like them:

Reason 1...

Boggler
had
big,
staring
eyes.

Reason 2...

Scratcher
had
sharp
claws.

Reason 3...

Howler had a loud,
screechy voice.

Meeeoooow!

Bonzo tried to scare the cats, but
the cats weren't scared of Bonzo.

Boggler sat on a gatepost and stared.

Scratcher put out her sharp claws.

Howler was so busy screeching
that she didn't even see him.

I'm just not scary enough,
Bonzo thought sadly.

Chapter Two

Big and Not-So-Big went to work.

Small went to school.

Tiny went to playgroup.

Bonzo made another list.

Bonzo practised being really scary. He went into the garden and barked at a snail ...

and a spider.

He barked at a bird ...

and a beetle.

They took no notice at all.

He barked at the
window cleaner.

The window cleaner laughed.

He barked at the postwoman.

She thought he was really friendly.

Bonzo went back to his basket.
He had done a lot of barking
but he hadn't scared anything.
I'm still not scary enough, Bonzo
thought sadly.

Chapter Three

That afternoon, Big and Not-So-Big came home. Tiny and Small came home too.

"Let's play football!" said Small.
They went into the garden.
Bonzo forgot about being scary.
He played really well.

He ran...

He tackled...

He headed...

He scored.

Then Small kicked the
ball very hard.

It went over the hedge, over the trees and ...

disappeared.

Bonzo ran after it. He squeezed through the hedge and into the wood. He sniffed and sniffed until he found the ball.

Then he spotted a sign
nailed to a tree.

Dr Fox was in.

Bonzo gave it a try. He stared
fiercely at a mouse.

He showed his teeth to
a hedgehog.

He chased a rabbit round the
park and down a hole.

He barked at some crows.
The crows took no notice.

"That's not loud enough,"
said Dr Fox.

"Louder still..." said Dr Fox.

"At last! I'm really scary now,"
said Bonzo. And he dribbled
the ball back home.

Chapter Four

When Bonzo and Small got home,
Big, Not-So-Big and Tiny were
standing in the garden. They were
looking into a box.

Bonzo sniffed.

Before Bonzo could stare fiercely,
the cat gave him a kiss.

Before Bonzo could show his teeth,
the cat purred and rubbed
against him.

Before Bonzo could chase her, the cat jumped on his tail.

Before Bonzo could bark loudly, the cat ran off with his ball.

And then, before Bonzo knew
what was happening, he was
playing football with the cat!

That night, Bonzo made
another list...

Things to do tomorrow:
1. Get out of bed
2. Say good morning TO THE CAT
3. Sniff around
4. Share breakfast WITH THE
    CAT
5. Go for a walk
6. Play football WITH THE CAT
7. Sleep

BONZO

Teensy-Weensy

He had MUCH better things to
do tomorrow than scaring cats!

For Danielle

First published 2005 by Walker Books Ltd
87 Vauxhall Walk, London SE11 5HJ

2 4 6 8 10 9 7 5 3 1

The right of Scoular Anderson to be identified as author
of this work has been asserted by him in accordance
with the Copyright, Designs and Patents Act 1988

This book has been typeset in Journal text

Handlettering by Scoular Anderson

Printed in China

British Library Cataloguing in Publication Data:
a catalogue record for this book is available
from the British Library

ISBN 1-84428-945-1

www.walkerbooks.co.uk